Disney FROZEN

Olaf
and the
Three Polar Bears

Designed by Scott Petrower and Whitney Manger
Illustrated by the Disney Storybook Art Team

Copyright © 2018 Disney Enterprises, Inc.
All rights reserved. Published by Disney Press, an imprint of Disney Book Group.
No part of this book may be reproduced or transmitted in any form or by any means,
electronic or mechanical, including photocopying, recording, or by any information storage
and retrieval system, without written permission from the publisher.
For information address
Disney Press, 1200 Grand Central Avenue, Glendale, California 91201.
Printed in the United States of America
First Hardcover Edition, October 2018
Library of Congress Control Number: 2017963707
1 3 5 7 9 10 8 6 4 2
FAC-038091-18250
ISBN 978-1-368-02140-1
For more Disney Press fun, visit www.disneybooks

Olaf
and the
Three Polar Bears

by Calliope Glass

DISNEP PRESS

LOS ANGELES • NEW YORK

Hello! It's Olaf, your favorite snowman! You're just in time to hear about that day I made some new friends who may have just been a dream but . . . Wait. I'm getting ahead of myself. Do you want to hear the story from the beginning?

You *do?*

Well . . .

Once upon a time, I was walking in the woods with my two friends Anna and Elsa, doing what I love most . . . smelling flowers.

Before I knew it, the two of them had wandered off!
They were probably lost and alone somewhere in the woods.
It's a good thing they had me to find them!

I called out their names, but all I heard was my own echo.

Just when I was about to turn back, I found a cottage! It was the most adorable little house I'd ever seen. Maybe I could meet some new friends who would help me find my old friends.

I knocked on the front door, and it swung open.
"Hello?" I called. "Is anybody home?"
But nobody answered.

"I guess maybe whoever lives here went out for a walk, too," I said.
"I bet they even met up with Anna and Elsa! This is perfect—I'll just
make myself comfortable and wait for them to come home."

HOME SWEET
➤ HOME ◄

While I was waiting, I smelled something really good and went to explore. In the kitchen, I found three bowls of porridge on the table. The **biggest** bowl smelled fishy to me, and the **middle**-sized bowl smelled a little too much like carrot—which is good for noses but not for porridge.

But the **little** bowl smelled the best—like summer and all things wonderful, with just a hint of cinnamon.

Smelling *is* one of my **favorite** things to do. Did you know that? Flowers, berries, even porridge— and that little bowl smelled amazing!

But when I picked it up—

AH AH AH

CHOO

I sneezed the bowl right out of my hands, and it shattered on the floor. I'll have to ask my new friends to make this for me again.

Wait! Speaking of friends, what was taking mine so long, anyway?

Since they weren't back yet, I grabbed my nose and continued exploring the cottage. There were three chairs in the living room—a **big** chair, a **MEDIUM** chair, and a **little** chair. I had a good idea of who my new friends were! One would give **big** hugs, one would give **MEDIUM** hugs, and the last one would probably give **little** hugs.

I tried to get into the **big** chair, but it was a little too tall for me. I managed to get on the MEDIUM chair, but it had too many cushions. So I plopped myself down in the **little** chair. It rocked just the right amount.

Aaaaaah.

So comfortable!

But I rocked too hard and–**whoops!**
All this waiting was getting exhausting. I needed to find a place to rest until my new friends came back with Anna and Elsa.

I kept walking around the little cottage, and soon I found the bedroom. There were even three beds to choose from! I tried each one, of course. The **big** bed smelled like fish, just like the big bowl of porridge. The **medium** bed was covered in fur. It felt like cuddling up with Sven, which is nice for a snuggle but not for a nap.

I got under the blanket in the **littlest** bed and it was so cozy,
it felt like a big hug from my friends.

I thought about how nice it would be to find them again, and maybe
go for a nice walk in the woods.

As I was thinking about my old friends and waiting for my new friends to come home, I decided to rest my eyes, just for a minute.

But while I was resting my eyes, my new friends came back!

As they made their way through the cottage, I'm sure
they were happy to find a new friend had come.

They came upstairs to find me—a cute, sweet, innocent little snowman snuggled under the covers in their bedroom!

I was so happy! My new friends weren't just any new friends—they were new friends who **loved** the snow as much as I did.

Because they were polar bears!
I jumped out of bed and ran so fast,
my legs could barely keep up.

That's when I ran into Anna and Elsa!
Maybe Elsa could make some snow for us all to
play in. Polar bears and snowmen love playing in
the snow. Did you know that?

"Where were you, Olaf?" Elsa cried. "We've been looking everywhere!"

"You'll never believe it!" I told them. "I found a little cottage, and it had yummy porridge, and a comfy chair, and a snuggly bed, and I met some new friends . . . and they're polar bears!"

Anna laughed. "Sounds like you had a dream, Olaf," she said.

Elsa smiled, too. "I think Anna's right."

Could it have been a dream? It had all seemed so real. The porridge, the bed . . . but then again . . .

"You know what," I said, "it probably *was* a dream."

That sure would explain a lot.

As we headed back to the castle, I shook my head. Silly Olaf! There never was a cottage with any polar bears after all.

Or was there?